P9-ASK-238

The Lighthouse Santa

SARA HOAGLAND HUNTER

Illustrated by JULIA MINER

University Press of New England

Hanover & London

Flying Dog Stories

Boston

For DOLLY SNOW BICKNELL,
the Lighthouse Santa's daughter,
& JEANETTE HASKINS KILLEN,
who grew up in the Great Point
Lighthouse

❄ SH

For LOUISA & KATELIN

❄ JM

University Press of New England
and Flying Dog Stories, an imprint of
New Horizons Partners
www.upne.com
Text © 2011 Sara Hoagland Hunter
Illustrations © 2011 Julia Miner
All rights reserved
Manufactured in China in April 2011
Production managed by O.G. Printing Productions,
Ltd., Kowloon, Hong Kong

For permission to reproduce any of the
material in this book, contact Permissions,
University Press of New England, One Court
Street, Suite 250, Lebanon NH 03766; or
visit www.upne.com

Library of Congress Cataloging-in-Publication Data
Hunter, Sara Hoagland.
The Lighthouse Santa / Sara Hoagland Hunter;
pictures by Julia Miner.
   p. cm.
"Flying dog stories."
Summary: Lighthouse keeper's daughter Kate
gets her Christmas wish when the Lighthouse Santa
drops in for a visit.
ISBN 978-1-61168-006-5 (cloth: alk. paper)
[1. Lighthouses — Fiction. 2. Santa Claus — Fiction.
3. Christmas — Fiction. 4. New England — Fiction.]
I. Miner, Julia, ill. II. Title.
PZ7.H9185Li   2011
[E] — dc22   2010052089

5 4 3 2 1

AUTHOR'S NOTE

Not long ago, the lighthouses dotting New England's coast were filled with children. Their Coast Guard fathers were assigned to keep the lights shining from Maine to Long Island. For a child stuck on an island outpost, life could be lonely. At no time were the feelings of isolation more severe than at Christmas. That is why, in 1936, a man named Edward Rowe Snow began his Christmas flights to the lighthouse children, dropping presents from his plane, the *Flying Santa*, for close to fifty years. The children who ran to the beaches and eagerly waited for their presents to drop from the sky are now grandparents. They still remember what it felt like to run for a brown paper package addressed to them from the Lighthouse Santa. Most lighthouses are automated now and Edward Rowe Snow is no longer alive, but the Flying Santa flights continue each Christmas in his honor.

I wait for the Lighthouse Santa. The wind roars. Windows rattle. Waves pound the shore and shake the house.

Sam says Santa won't come tonight because of the storm at sea.

But Dad promises, "Nothing is impossible on Christmas Eve in a lighthouse."

The Lighthouse Santa drops presents to all of us who live alone at the edge of the ocean. From Owl's Head Light in Maine to our Great Point Light on Nantucket, we wait for the sound of his plane. He has never missed a Christmas . . . at least, not yet.

"He's not coming, Kate," says Sam. "No plane can fly in weather like this. It's snowing too hard to see the lighthouse."

But I know he'll see it. I polished the lens myself this morning. It shines on Cross Rip and Tuckernuck shoals where so many ships have crashed. My father watches from the tower, making sure the light will not blow out.

"What did you wish for?" I ask my brother.

"A razor to shave with," mumbles Sam.

I giggle. That's what the Lighthouse Santa drops for Dad each year. Sam's only thirteen and has no whiskers.

"What's so funny?" asks Sam. "What did *you* wish for?"
I'm bursting to tell him but I'm afraid if I do, it won't come true.
"Probably something impossible, as usual," says Sam.
But I know nothing is impossible on Christmas Eve in a lighthouse.

When I wake in the night, my father is shouting.

"What's wrong?" I call.

"Shipwreck!" says Sam, yanking on his foul weather gear.

"Hush!" says my mother. "We don't know that yet. Your father thought he saw a light beyond the far dunes. The phone is out so we're not sure what's happening."

Dad grabs a lantern while Mom ties Sam's scarf extra tight. Snow swirls in the kitchen, knocking the tide chart off the wall as Sam and my father are swallowed by the night.

All I can think of are the 51 shipwrecks in the lighthouse logbook and the people who froze like popsicles to the rigging. "Will Dad and Sam be all right?"

"Of course," says my mother, boiling pots of coffee and grabbing quilts to heat in front of the stove.

The wind sounds like a thousand seagulls shrieking. Suddenly there is a THUMP! Mom and I jump. It's only Moby.

"Let's sing Christmas carols," says my mother, wrapping me in a quilt. I bury my face in Moby's fur so I can't see the waves crash outside our front door.

"Noel, Noel, Noel, Noel," sings Mom.

No Dad, no Sam, no Santa, no wish coming true.

On and on she sings to drown out the wind: "Jingle Bells" and "We Three Kings" and "Good King Wenceslas". . . until there is a pounding at the door.

In blows Sam — frozen from his scarf to his eyelashes.

"Quick, Kate! The quilts!" says Mother. A frozen man follows Sam, stomping snow from his boots. His beard drips with icicles. "Come in!" says my mother, dragging him to the stove.

Next, my father stumbles in holding a pile of snowy blankets. When I leap to hug him, the pile moves! A red cap with a white fur pom-pom wiggles to the top. Suddenly, I am face to face with a girl just my size.

"Who are you?" is all I can think to say.

"She's the Lighthouse Santa's daughter and I rescued her!" announces Sam.

The man with the icicle beard reaches to shake my hand. His voice is as soothing as honey on snowflakes.

"I'm Mr. Snow, the Lighthouse Santa, and this is Dolly. You must be Kate. I hear you're a big help with the lighthouse."

Could he really be here in our kitchen? Why didn't anyone tell me the Lighthouse Santa had a daughter my age?

12

Dad unwraps Dolly and places her in my rocking chair.

Mr. Snow answers questions while I pour mugs of hot chocolate.

"When the wings iced up, we had to land at the airport," he says. "I borrowed a truck and made it to the families at Brant Point Light and Sankaty Head. I wasn't sure we should risk the trip way out here but . . ."

13

"We wanted your family to have your presents!" cries out Dolly.

"We got stuck in the dunes," says Mr. Snow. "We were lucky somebody polished that light so bright or we never would have found you," he says, smiling right at me.

Dolly and I toast marshmallows while Mr. Snow spins stories of sailors and lighthouses from Maine to Massachusetts.

When my eyes start to droop, Mom allows us one carol before bed. Dolly and I request "Silent Night." Sam groans. But for once, he is outnumbered.

"Do you have a nightlight?" Dolly whispers as we climb the stairs.
"Only the biggest one in the world!"
"Wow!" says Dolly, as she sees the lighthouse glow.
We talk until we fall asleep. Dolly tells me about a neighborhood I can hardly imagine — where kids wait at a bus stop and ride bikes all together. I tell her about our Fourth of July clambake and how to catch a bluefish. "You're lucky to live in a lighthouse," Dolly says.
But I think I am even luckier that my Christmas wish is coming true.

17

In the morning, the storm is over. The sun is so squinty bright, I wake up early. "Hey, Dolly," I whisper. "Want to be first to the lighthouse?"

Dolly jumps out of bed. We trudge through the snow and count all 157 steps together.

"MERRY CHRISTMAS!" we shout to the gulls.

"MERRY CHRISTMAS!" we shout to the seal floating by on an ice floe.

On the way to dig out the truck, we teach Dolly how to dune sled. When Sam pretends to be a surfer, we skid over the frozen marsh and crash in a pile.

Too soon, it is time for the ride to town.

"Would you like your gifts delivered by hand or the old-fashioned way?" asks Mr. Snow.

"Air mail as usual!" answers Sam.

Dolly promises to write me a letter. I want to tell her I hope she'll visit again but the words stick in my throat.

"Would you like to help us deliver the last few presents, Kate?" asks Mr. Snow.

Would I?!

All of Nantucket spreads out beneath us as we climb higher than ten lighthouses. The ferry looks like a toy boat tied to a matchstick dock. First drop — Martha's Vineyard. We circle West Chop Lighthouse where the Cummings family has stomped "Merry Christmas" in the snow. Freezing air fills the cabin as the Lighthouse Santa tosses five bundles to the children waiting below.

Next drop is Cuttyhunk Island where a giant wreath hangs from the lighthouse railing and our bundles just miss the pond.

"Last stop coming up!" says Mr. Snow, heading for Great Point. "It's your turn, Kate! There's a razor for your dad, one of my pirate books for Sam, and fresh coffee for your mother."

I take a moment to switch the names on Dad's and Sam's gifts.

Soon, we are circling the lighthouse I know so well, waving to Mom, Dad, and Moby. Sam waits below, wearing a helmet. *Very funny*.

The wind pulls at the package in my mitten. "Now!" cries Mr. Snow. I drop one, then two, then three bundles to the beach. "Congratulations! Perfect shot!" he says. "Now, how about a book or a doll for my favorite lighthouse keeper?"

When I shake my head no, Dolly looks worried. "But that's all we have to give you, Kate."

24

"Don't you know the Lighthouse Santa already brought exactly what I wished for?" I say.

"He did?" she asks.

I nod. "All I ever wanted was a friend."

Dolly smiles. "Can Kate fly with us again next year, Dad? Can we stay at her lighthouse?"

The Lighthouse Santa winks and answers, "Nothing is impossible on Christmas Eve in a lighthouse."